SCHOOL BUS
OF HORRORS

SHOCKS!

HELP!
ME!

D1364420

raintree
a Capstone company — publishers for children

Raintree is an imprint of Capstone Global Library Limited, a company incorporated
in England and Wales having its registered office at 264 Banbury Road, Oxford, OX2
7DY – Registered company number: 6695582

www.raintree.co.uk
myorders@raintree.co.uk

Designed by Sarah Bennett
Original illustrations © Capstone Global Library Limited 2019
Cover background by Shutterstock/oldmonk
Production by Tori Abraham
Originated by Capstone Global Library Ltd
Printed and bound in India

ISBN 978 1 4747 6912 9
23 22 21 20 19
10 9 8 7 6 5 4 3 2 1

British Library Cataloguing in Publication Data
A full catalogue record for this book is available from the British Library.

CONTENTS

From dawn to dusk, the **SCHOOL BUS OF HORRORS** rumbles along city streets and down country roads, searching for another passenger. Yellow, black markings, dirty windows – it looks like any other school bus.

But **BEWARE!** Step aboard this bus and

experience the scariest ride of your life . . .

CHAPTER ONE
SHOCKING

Lightning flashes.

The sky flickers like a TV screen controlled by zombies.

Hari holds his bag above his head to avoid the rain. It doesn't help.

He is the only person at this
bus stop.

It's just him, a mailbox and a
billboard at the end of a lonely road.

Storm clouds turn the sky as dark as night.

Hari can see the old billboard only when there is a flash of lightning.

The billboard has been blank for as long as Hari has lived here.

Lightning flashes again.
Hari wipes rain from his eyes.

Suddenly electric lights glow on the billboard!

The blue lights read:

TROUBLE WITH YOUR SHOCKS?

DON'T DELAY!

COME TO

SKELTON'S MOTORS

TODAY!

Lightning flashes above the billboard.

"Shocks?" Hari says out loud.

Hari hears a rumble on the road.

Then he sees dim headlights glowing in the pouring rain.

The bus, thinks Hari. *Finally.*

Rain covers the road like a sheet of plastic.

Hari's shoes are as wet as his bag.

SKKKREEEECH!

The bus driver hits the brakes. The powerful wheels slip on the wet road.

RREEEERRRRRRK!

The bus doesn't stop. It swerves sideways as it comes towards Hari and the mailbox.

Hari stands frozen. He closes his eyes and waits for the impact.

CHAPTER THREE
FAMILIAR

KA-RAAAK!

Another flash of lightning crashes through the dark.

Hari blinks. He is suddenly sitting on the bus in his usual seat.

It is not his usual bus.

He sees only the driver at the front. The driver sits behind a thick plastic wall.

Where is everyone? Hari wonders.

"Hari!" comes a familiar voice.

Hari turns around and sees an old woman sitting at the back of the bus.

"Grandma!" shouts Hari.

Hari runs to the woman and hugs her tightly.

"What are you doing here?" asks Hari. "You're–"

Dead, Hari thinks.

"Oh, Hari," says Grandma. "I have something for you."

She holds a brown box.

"I hope you can use it," Grandma adds with a smile.

"Grandma, how did you get here?" asks Hari.

"What do you mean, dear?" she asks. "You seem shocked to see me."

CHAPTER FOUR
THE GIFT

WOOF! WOOF!

Two dogs run down the aisle of the bus towards Hari.

"Buddy and Holly!" cries Hari. He hasn't seen his dogs in a long time.

But they're dead too, he thinks.

"Grandma," says Hari. "Does this
mean that I'm—?"

"They love you so much, don't they?" says Grandma. She bends down to stroke the dogs.

"Now open your present," she adds.

Inside the brown box is a new leather rucksack.

"Wow!" says Hari. "But it's not my birthday."

The old woman looks at him strangely.

"I thought you might need a new one soon," she says. "You can thank me later."

Lightning flashes right outside the bus windows. The bus's lights go off and on.

Hari screams.

The old woman has changed.

She is a skeleton in an old dress. A few hairs grow from her skull.

"Don't you like your present, Hari?" asks the skeleton. "The shop assistant said the bag is waterproof."

CHAPTER FIVE
NOT GONE

The sky rumbles and lightning flashes again.

Hari is standing at the bus stop, holding his bag over his head.

He lowers the bag and looks around.

He ignores the falling rain soaking his clothes.

"Grandma?" says Hari weakly.

He looks down, hoping to see his old dogs. But he is alone again at the bus stop.

SKKKREEEECH!

A school bus appears on the road.
The powerful wheels slip and slide.

The huge vehicle roars towards
Hari.

Electric lights flash on the billboard again.

One word blinks on and off: TROUBLE.

KKTAAANG!

The mailbox is struck and flies through the air.

Just as the bus swings near him, Hari jumps.

The bus swerves and crashes into the billboard.

Hari stands, frozen.

He can see his bag. It is crushed under one of the wheels of the bus.

Then he feels a weight on his shoulders. He is wearing a leather rucksack.

Harry looks at the storm clouds overhead. "Thanks, Grandma," he says.

GLOSSARY

aisle path that runs between seats on a bus
billboard outdoor sign used to advertise products
familiar well known or easily recognized
impact striking of one thing against another
swerve change direction quickly, usually to avoid something

DISCUSS

1. Why do you think this book is called *Shocks!*?

2. Do you think Hari actually met his grandmother on the bus, or did he imagine the whole thing? Use clues from the story to support your answer.

3. What is your favourite illustration in this book? Describe why it's your favourite.

WRITE

1. Create a new title for this book. Then write a paragraph on why you chose your new title.

2. Write a story about a storm that you've experienced. If you can't think of a real-life storm, make one up!

3. Write about the scariest bus journey you've ever experienced.

AUTHOR

MICHAEL DAHL is the author of the Library of Doom series, the Dragonblood books and Michael Dahl's Really Scary Stories. (He wants everyone to know that last title was not his idea.) He was born a few minutes after midnight of April Fool's Day in a thunderstorm, has survived various tornados and hurricanes, as well as an attack from a rampant bunny at night ("It reared up at me!"). He currently lives in a haunted house and once saw a ghost in his high school. He will never travel on a school bus. These stories will explain why.

ILLUSTRATOR

EUAN COOK is an illustrator from London, who enjoys drawing pictures for books and watching foxes and jays out of his window. He also likes walking around looking at broken brickwork, sooty statues and the weird drainpipes and stuff you can find behind old run-down buildings.

SCHOOL BUS OF HORRORS

AUTO BODY PARTS

NIGHT SHIFT

OOZE CONTROL

SHOCKS!

CRUSH HOUR

DEAD END

DESTRUCTION ZONE

FRIDAY NIGHT HEADLIGHTS

THE SQUEALS ON THE BUS

UNDER THE BONNET